The Tortoise
and the Funfair

Written by
Harry Norton

Illustrated by
Tom Fisk

There once was a tortoise, who was just a normal guy – he definitely wasn't a superhero who knew how to fly...

He was out with friends at the fair one night; playing games and eating goodies that filled them with delight.

The tortoise and his friends went on loads of cool rides — upside-down rollercoasters and two giant slides.

But his favourite game of all was called 'Hook-a-Duck'; the tortoise just hoped that he'd have some good luck!

He managed to hook one as quick as a flash – so quick in fact, it gave them a splash!

His friends all hurried him to check if he'd won – to do that he'd have to look at the bum!

As he turned it over he was no longer cheerful, his mood had changed to one which was fearful...

Of all the ducks that were sat their afloat, the tortoise had picked the one with the goat!

All of a sudden, the funfair turned dark – this wasn't supposed to happen tonight in the park!

In the blink of an eye, the tortoise ran away – he knew that he would have to save the day.

Once the tortoise had found somewhere quiet, he knew that it was now time to try it...

He pulled a red button from out of his pocket, which would send his suit to him like a rocket.

In just a few seconds, the suit did appear – including some awesome, brand new headgear.

All suited up, it was now time to go.

"Get ready baddie, it's time for the show!"

Flying through the air at the speed of sound, the tortoise arrived back, safely landing on the ground.

But the fair was now still, void of all noise – it was weird seeing no one playing with the toys...

Wandering around the funfair, the tortoise began to feel, that whoever caused this, could be atop the Ferris Wheel.

So he flew up there as quick as a flash, and soon after, he found a secret stash...

You see, in one of the seats there was a ton of money – but in another there was a poor, tied-up bunny!

Tied up too were his friends just below, but when he went to free them, he was hit by a blow!

"Ha, ha!" an evil voice said with a chuckle.

"How do you like the taste of my knuckle?!"

With that powerful hit, our friend fell to the ground; but he was soon back to his feet – he wasn't messing around!

He looked to the wheel again and saw the goat with his loot. His friends all shouted,

"Quick, stop him, shoot!"

But with all the dark clouds it was too hard to see; does this mean the goat got away free?!

No, because the money and treasures kept making a clang, which allowed our friend the tortoise to use his boomerang!

The tortoise listened carefully and then took a guess, launching his weapon – which ended in success.

The special boomerang wrapped around the bad guy, which sent the evil goat down from the sky...

The baddie landed with a huge splash; but dry and safe was all of the cash!

The villain landed with the ducks still afloat...

Allowing the police to play 'Hook-a-Goat'!

Other books in this series:

The Tortoise and the Lair

33977352R00021

Printed in Poland
by Amazon Fulfillment
Poland Sp. z o.o., Wrocław